PETER P

Peter Potts is everyone
driving her mad. Mrs H
while the school's blocked gutter is making everyone wet
when they come inside. With Clarence, his parrot, to wake him
up in the mornings, life for Peter is never dull. This collection
of eight delightful stories full of Peter Potts' adventures is
guaranteed to amuse and entertain all young readers.

Margaret Ryan was born in Paisley in Scotland and now lives
in Greenock with her husband. She has two children and was a
teacher before she became a writer full time.

By the same author

GRISELDA F.G.M.

Margaret Ryan

Peter Potts
The Plumber

Illustrated by
Caroline Crossland

PUFFIN BOOKS

PUFFIN BOOKS

Published by the Penguin Group
Penguin Books Ltd, 27 Wrights Lane, London W8 5TZ, England
Penguin Books USA Inc., 375 Hudson Street, New York, New York 10014, USA
Penguin Books Australia Ltd, Ringwood, Victoria, Australia
Penguin Books Canada Ltd, 10 Alcorn Avenue, Toronto, Ontario, Canada M4V 3B2
Penguin Books (NZ) Ltd, 182–190 Wairau Road, Auckland 10, New Zealand

Penguin Books Ltd, Registered Offices: Harmondsworth, Middlesex, England

First published by Viking 1992
Published in Puffin Books 1993
1 3 5 7 9 10 8 6 4 2

Printed in England by Clays Ltd, St Ives plc
Filmset in Palatino

To John, Susie and Jonathan, with love

Contents

Peter Potts
and the Leaky Tap

Peter Potts the plumber was having a
lovely dream. He dreamed he was fixing
all the leaky taps in Buckingham Palace.
He was just chatting to the Queen about
spanners when there was the sound of a
telephone ringing.

POORP POORP. POORP POORP.

"Answer that, would you, Mr Potts,"
said the Queen.

Mr Potts reached out and picked up his own bedside telephone. "Potts's Plumbers, by appointment to the Queen," he said.

There was no answer. Then . . .

"POORP POORP. POORP POORP. TIME TO GET UP. TIME TO GET UP," squawked Mr Potts's parrot, Clarence.

Grumpily Mr Potts got out of bed. Clarence always spoiled his best dreams. He was just climbing into his big blue overalls when the phone really did ring. Mr Potts picked it up.

"Potts's plumbing services. Can I help you?"

"Oh, I hope so," said the voice at the other end. "My name is Mrs Munro, and I have a leaky tap in my kitchen. It's going DRIP DRIP, DROP DROP, DRIP DRIP, and the noise is driving me mad."

"I'll be over right away, madam," said Mr Potts, and he put on his baseball cap, picked up his big bag of tools and set off in his little red van.

"Oh, I'm so glad you're here," said Mrs Munro when he arrived. "My tap's got worse. Instead of going DRIP DRIP, DROP DROP, DRIP DRIP, it's now going TINK TINK, TANK TANK, TINK TINK. And the noise is driving me *really* mad."

"Don't you worry, Mrs Munro," said Mr Potts. "I'll soon fix it for you. Show me the way to the kitchen."

Mrs Munro led the way and, sure enough, there was the leaky tap going TINK TINK, TANK TANK, TINK TINK.

"I can sort that out soon enough," said Mr Potts, getting out a big spanner. "It just needs a little adjusting, that's all. There we are . . . It's stopped."

"Oh, thank you, Mr Potts. That's much better," said Mrs Munro. "I'll just see you out now."

They had only got as far as the front door, though, when they heard a noise. It went PLIP PLIP, PLOP PLOP, PLIP PLIP. "Oh no," said Mrs Munro. "Not that tap again."

"Leave this to me," said Mr Potts, going back to the kitchen. "It just needs a little more adjusting." He got out a bigger spanner and adjusted the tap a little more.

"There we are," he said. "That's fixed it this time."

Sure enough, the tap was quiet.

Mr Potts gathered up his big bag of tools and went to the front door. He stopped and listened. All was silent. He smiled and opened the door. Then he heard it. SPLISH SPLISH, SPLASH SPLASH, SPLISH SPLISH.

"I don't believe it," he shouted to Mrs Munro. "Well, that tap's not going to get the better of me. I'm going to fix it once and for all." And he took out of his tool-bag the biggest spanner he had. He strode back into the kitchen and adjusted the tap as far as it would go. Then he stood back, red in the face.

"There now, Mrs Munro. That's fixed it good and proper. It won't give you any more trouble, or my name's not Peter Potts."

"Oh, thank you very much, Mr Potts. You've been so helpful. I'll just see you out now."

13

Mr Potts got to the front door and stopped and listened. All was quiet. He opened the front door. All was still quiet. He smiled. That tap knew when it was beaten. He turned to say cheerio to Mrs Munro. Then he heard it. PITTER PITTER, PATTER PATTER, PITTER PITTER.

Mr Potts got so mad he took off his baseball cap and threw it on to the floor.

Then he took a big heavy hammer from his tool-bag and marched into the kitchen.

"I'm going to fix that tap if it's the last thing I do," he cried as he ran over to the kitchen sink. He lifted his big hammer above his head . . . then stopped. The tap was silent. No DRIPS or DROPS. No TINKS or TANKS. No PLIPS or PLOPS. Not even any SPLISHES or SPLASHES. Mr Potts put down his hammer and scratched his head.

"I don't understand it, Mrs Munro," he said. "I definitely heard a PITTER PITTER, PATTER PATTER, PITTER PITTER. Didn't you?"

"Yes," said Mrs Munro. "But I knew it wasn't the tap this time."

"What is it, then?"

"Look out of the window, Mr Potts, and you'll see."

"Oh no," said Mr Potts. "It's raining!"

Peter Potts and the Chilly Day

One chilly morning Peter Potts the plumber opened one eye and looked at his bedroom window. Patterns of frost covered the pane.

"Brrrrr," he said. "It's too cold to get up. I think I'll just turn over." And he did. The wrong way. And fell out of bed.

"TIME TO GET UP. TIME TO GET UP," squawked Clarence, the parrot.

"I am up," muttered Mr Potts. "And perhaps I'd better stay up. There will be a lot of work for me to do with this cold weather."

"IN COLD WEATHER," squawked Clarence, "WEAR A JUMPER, A JACKET AND A SCARF."

"I know, I know," said Mr Potts, and he
put on his big blue overalls, his baseball
cap, a green jumper, a brown jacket and a
red scarf. He was just picking up his big
bag of tools when the doorbell rang. It was
Jemima Sweet, the policewoman.

"Oh, Peter," she cried, "can you come quickly? There's a burst pipe in my house and there's water everywhere."

Peter hurried to Jemima's house. In the hall some large drips were coming through the ceiling. They dripped PLOP PLOP on to Peter Potts's baseball cap; they dripped PLIP PLIP on to Jemima Sweet's police hat; they even dripped PLOP PLIP on to the large black nose of Hairy Sweet, the sheep-dog.

"RUFF, VERY RUFF," barked Hairy, and wiped his nose on the carpet.

Mr Potts set to work. He turned off the water, then climbed up into the loft.

"Oh dear, oh dear, you know what you've got here, don't you?" he said to Mrs Sweet.

"Leaky pipes?"

"COLD leaky pipes," said Mr Potts, fixing the leak. "Pipes are like people – they need to be covered up in cold weather. I'll cover this one with my scarf for the moment." And he took off his long red scarf and wound it round the pipe.

He was just saying cheerio to Jemima when hurrying down the street came Enoch Twyce, the postman.

"Oh, Peter," he cried, "can you come quickly? There's a burst water tank in my house and there's water everywhere."

Peter hurried to Enoch's house. In the kitchen large drips were coming through the ceiling. They dripped SPLISH SPLISH on to Peter Potts's baseball cap;

they dripped SPLOSH SPLOSH on to Enoch Twyce's postman's hat; they even dripped SPLISH SPLOSH on to the stripy head of Emu Twyce, the kitten.

"MEE OW, MEE WET," he squeaked, and wiped his head on the curtains.

Mr Potts set to work. He turned off the water, then climbed up into the loft.

"Oh dear, oh dear, you know what you've got here, don't you?" he said to Mr Twyce.

"A leaky tank?"

"A COLD leaky tank," said Mr Potts, fixing the leak. "Tanks are like people – they need to be covered up in cold weather. I'll cover this one with my jacket for the moment." And he took off his big

brown jacket and fastened it round the
water tank.

He was just saying cheerio to Enoch
when hurrying down the street came Susie
Lee, the district nurse.

"Oh, Peter," she said, "can you come
quickly? There's a burst drain-pipe outside
my house and there's water everywhere."

Peter hurried to Susie's house, where

large squirts of water were coming through the drain-pipe. They squirted SPLID SPLID on to Peter Potts's baseball cap; they squirted SPLUD SPLUD on to Susie Lee's nurse's hat; they even squirted SPLID SPLUD on to the shiny tummy of Gordon, the garden gnome, but he just carried on fishing.

"Oh dear, oh dear," said Mr Potts. "I'll have to go back home and get some special stuff to fix that pipe, but for the moment I'll stop the leak with this." And he took off his green woolly jumper and wrapped it round the drain-pipe.

Then he hurried home. By now he was shivering.

"IN COLD WEATHER," squawked Clarence, "WEAR A JUMPER, A JACKET AND A SCARF."

"I know, I know," said Mr Potts, "and before I go back outside, I'm going to have a hot cup of tea."

He made the tea and tried to pour in the milk. It wouldn't pour.

"That's funny," said Mr Potts, and squeezed the carton. It felt very hard. "Oh no," said Mr Potts, "now the milk's frozen. Perhaps I'll have to wrap that up as well."

Peter Potts and the Smelly Drain

It was a beautiful sunny morning, but Peter Potts was still asleep. Though not for long. Clarence, his parrot, decided to sing.

"Good morning, Mr Sun, tra-la, it's time to have some fun, tra-la . . ."

Mr Potts pulled a pillow over his head.

"It's going to be a lovely day . . ."

Mr Potts pulled two pillows over his head.

"Parrots and plumbers come out to play . . ."

Mr Potts threw both pillows at Clarence and got up. He knew when he was beaten. He was just climbing into his big blue overalls and putting on his baseball cap when the telephone rang.

"Potts's plumbing services. Can I help you?"

"I hope so," said a gruff voice at the other end. "This is Farmer McDonald. I have a very smelly drain in my farmyard and it's upsetting the animals. Will you come and have a look at it?"

"Right away," said Mr Potts, and he set off in his little red van.

In no time at all, he had arrived at Farmer McDonald's farm.

"Oh dear, oh dear," said Mr Potts, getting out of his van and holding his nose. "You have got a nasty smell there."

The animals agreed.

"BAAAAD BAAAAD," said the sheep, shaking their heads.

"PHOOOO PHOOOO," said the cows, wrinkling their nostrils.

"COR BLIMEY," said the crows, and flew up into the trees.

"I'll just get my rods out of the van and give the drain a poke," said Mr Potts.

"Aha, what have we here?" he said, working with his rods. And he pulled out of the drain something that went JINGLE JANGLE JINGLE, JINGLE JANGLE JINGLE.

"Why, those are the spare keys for my big tractor," said Farmer McDonald. "I wonder how they got down the drain."

"Some very funny things get down drains," said Mr Potts. "But that's not what's causing the smell." And he poked his rods back down again, a bit deeper.

"Aha, what have we here?" he said. And he pulled out of the drain something that went HONK HINK HONK, HONK HINK HONK.

"Why, that's the horn from my big tractor," said Farmer McDonald. "I wonder how it got down the drain."

"Some very funny things get down drains," said Mr Potts. "But that's not what's causing the smell." And he poked his rods back down again, deeper still.

"There's something else here," he said. "If I can just reach it."

"I hope it's not my big tractor," said Farmer McDonald. "I'm not too sure where I left it."

But it wasn't the big tractor. It was two long, brown, soggy things that went SLURP SQUIDGE PLOP, SLURP SQUIDGE PLOP.

"Why, these are my muck-spreading socks," cried Farmer McDonald. "So that's where they went. I've been looking for them for ages." And he picked them up and waved them in the air to dry.

"BAAAAD BAAAAD," said the sheep, and trotted off.

"PHOOOO PHOOOO," said the cows, and galloped away.

And all the crows got into a flap and gave a nasty CORF CORF.

"Now I wonder how on earth these socks got down that drain," said Farmer McDonald.

"Probably walked on their own," said Mr Potts. And he too walked away. Quickly.

Peter Potts and the Windy Day

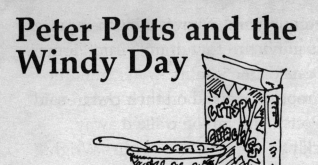

One windy morning while Mr Potts was eating his bowl of Crispy Crackles, CRISP CRISP CRACK, and Clarence was cracking open pistachio nuts with his beak, CRACK CRACK GOTCHA, the telephone rang.

"Pttts's plmmmmming servvvvvvs," said Mr Potts through a mouthful of Crackles. "Can I hpppppp you?"

"Pardon?" said the voice at the other end.

Mr Potts swallowed ULLLLLLP fast. "Potts's plumbing services," he said. "Can I help you?"

"Oh, it *is* you, Mr Potts," said the voice. "It's Miss Wright from the children's playgroup here. There's a blocked gutter right above the playgroup's front door, and every time it rains, water from the gutter pours down on to the children. I wonder if you can help?"

"I'll be over right away, Miss Wright," said Mr Potts, and he put on his baseball cap and collected his big bag of tools. He was just getting into his little red van when Enoch Twyce the postman arrived with a long thin parcel for him. "Thanks, Enoch," said Mr Potts, putting it into his van. "I won't open it now. I know what's inside."

Then he zoomed off to the playgroup.

When he got there, the children and Miss Wright were in the garden, playing chasing games.

"Come and play with us, Mr Potts," they called.

"Right," said Mr Potts, and he laid down his big bag of tools. First they played boys chase girls, then they played girls chase boys. After that they played chase the woolly hat as a big gust of wind came and whirled it off Miss Wright's head, sending it round and round the garden.

Then, while the children and Miss

Wright watched, Mr Potts got on with his work. He got out a long ladder from the back of his little red van and set it up by the front door. Then he climbed up and up and up till he reached the very top. He leaned over and had a look in the gutter.

"Aha," he said, "what have we here?" And he took out a flat red object and sent it spinning WHEEEEEE through the air.

"Why, it's the playgroup's frisbee," said Miss Wright, as it landed at her feet. "I wondered where that had gone."

While the children had a good game with the frisbee, Mr Potts had another look in the gutter.

"Aha, aha," he said, "what have we here?" And he took out two round yellow objects and sent them spinning WHEEEEEE WHEEEEEE through the air.

"Why, they're the playgroup's tennis balls," said Miss Wright, as they landed at her feet. "I wondered where they had gone."

While the children had a good game with the tennis balls, Mr Potts had yet another look in the gutter.

"Aha, aha, aha," he said, "what have we here?" This time he didn't send anything spinning through the air, but climbed back down the ladder instead.

"There's a bird's nest up there," he told everyone, "with three baby birds in it. Now, I can't clear the nest till the babies have grown up a bit and flown away, so I tell you what I'll do . . ."

He went to the back of his little red van and took out the long thin parcel Enoch Twyce the postman had delivered that morning. "Look inside," said Mr Potts.

Miss Wright and the children opened the parcel. Inside was a large umbrella with bowls of Crispy Crackles painted all over it.

"I saved up my box-tops for it," said Mr Potts. "So that'll keep you dry till I can clear the gutter properly."

The children laughed and put up the umbrella. That was a mistake. A very big gust of wind came and blew it . . . WHOOOOOOSH . . . up into the air. Up into the gutter.

Atishoo, Peter Potts

One morning Peter Potts the plumber woke up with a terrible cold. He couldn't even hear the news on the radio, his head ached so much . . . G-THUMP G-THUMP; his ears ached so much . . . B-DOING B-DOING; and his nose dripped . . . DRIP DRIP DRIP DRIP DRIP . . . constantly.

"I wish I could stay in bed this morning," he said to Clarence. "But I've got a long list of customers to see. I hate catching a head cold."

"FOR A HEAD COLD," squawked Clarence, "WEAR A WOOLLY HAT. WEAR A WOOLLY HAT."

"That's not a bad idea, Clarence," said Mr Potts, climbing into his big blue overalls. "I'll wear a woolly hat to keep my head warm, put some cotton wool in my aching ears, and take an extra-large hanky to blow my drippy nose."

When he was ready, Mr Potts picked up his big bag of tools and set off in his little red van with his list of customers.

He went to see Mrs Jones who lived near the waterworks first. She had a leaky bath.

"Good morning, Mr Potts," she said when he arrived. "I'm surprised to see you just now. You must know you won't be able to find the leak this morning. Can you come back this afternoon?"

"What?" said Mr Potts, who could hardly hear a thing with his head aching

G-THUMP G-THUMP. "Come back with a balloon? It's not a plumber you need, it's a clown."

And he stomped off back to his van.

He checked his list and drove round the corner to his next customer. It was Mr Brown. He had a leaky shower-head.

"Good morning, Mr Potts," said Mr Brown when the plumber arrived. "I'm surprised to see you just now. You must know you won't be able to find the leak this morning. Can you come back this afternoon?"

"What?" said Mr Potts, who could hardly hear a thing with his ears aching B-DOING B-DOING. "Come back with a bassoon? It's not a plumber you need, it's a musician."

And he stomped off back to his van.

He checked his list and drove down the street to his next customer. It was Miss Smith. She had a leaky garden-tap.

"Good morning, Mr Potts," she said when he arrived. "I'm surprised to see you just now. You must know you won't be able to find the leak this morning. Can you come back this afternoon?"

"What?" said Mr Potts, who could hardly hear a thing with his nose dripping . . . DRIP DRIP DRIP DRIP DRIP . . . constantly. "Come back with a baboon? It's not a plumber you need, it's a zoo-keeper."

And he stomped off back to his van.

The next customer on his list *was* a zoo-keeper. Fred was washing Hannibal, the elephant, with water from a

kettle when Mr Potts arrived.

"Don't worry about Hannibal, Fred," said Mr Potts, getting out his bag of tools. "I'll soon get the tap in the elephant house working, and you can give Hannibal his proper bath."

"But you must know you won't be able to fix it till this afternoon," said Fred.

"Fix it with a spoon?" said Mr Potts, taking off his woolly hat, taking out his woolly ear-plugs and taking out his extra-big hanky to give his drippy nose a good blow. "I don't know what's gone wrong with everyone this morning, talking about spoons and baboons and balloons and bassoons. I wish I'd stayed in bed with my cold."

"You should have," said Fred. "Didn't you hear the news on the radio? There's a problem with the town's new waterworks, and all the water's been turned off till this afternoon. You won't be able to find any leaks till then."

"Right," said Mr Potts, getting back into

his little red van. "I'm off then."

"Where are you going in such a hurry?" asked Fred.

"Back to my bed," said Mr Potts.
BROOOOOM BROOOOOM
BROOOOOM BROOOOOM
BROOOOOM.

Good Morning, Peter Potts

One morning Mr Potts woke up without any help from Clarence because the parrot was still asleep.

"Well, fancy that," said Mr Potts. "Just look at the time, and that parrot hasn't woken me up yet. If he doesn't wake me soon, I'll be late for work. Maybe I'd better wake him instead, this morning. No, wait a minute. I know what I'll do. I'll make as much noise as I can. I'll clatter and bang about and see how he likes it, when he's trying to sleep."

Mr Potts got out of bed, put on his big blue overalls and his baseball cap, and went to bring in the milk. On the step were two squashy cartons.

Mr Potts picked them up.

"Huh," he said, "can't make much noise with these."

Just then one carton burst open and the cold milk ran in fat rivers down the legs of the big blue overalls and into Mr Potts's teddy-bear slippers.

FLAP SLAP FLAP went the soggy blue trouser legs.

SQUODGE SQUIDGE SQUODGE went the teddy-bear slippers.

Mr Potts changed into a dry pair of big blue overalls and put on his pink baseball boots.

"Now where's that noisy breakfast cereal?" he said. "The one that goes SLAP, QUACKLE and PLOP. I'll have some of that."

He emptied some into a huge bowl, poured on some milk and listened . . . Nothing . . . No noise at all. Not even a WHISSSSSSSSPER.

"That's very strange," said Mr Potts, and he put his ear right down to the bowl.

BOO went the cereal.

"EEK," went Mr Potts.

GLOOG GLOOG GLUG went the baseball cap as it fell off Mr Potts's head and landed in the bowl.

Mr Potts rescued his cap and put it on the radiator to dry. "This is all Clarence's fault," he said. "If he'd woken me up when he should have, this wouldn't have happened. I wonder if he's awake yet."

He poked his head round the bedroom door and had a look. Clarence was sitting there on his perch, his head tucked underneath his wing, still asleep. Just then, there were two loud knocks on the front door KNOCK KNOCK.

Mr Potts opened the door and found Enoch Twyce the postman standing there.

"I hope I didn't get you out of bed, Peter," said Enoch. "But there's a parcel for you."

Mr Potts went back to the kitchen and opened up the parcel.

"Great," he said, "the special hammer I ordered. Now I can put up my picture of the town's new waterworks. I'll do that straight away. I'll hammer a nail in the wall above my bed. Clarence won't sleep through that noise."

He went into the bedroom and started to put up the picture.

BANG HAMMER OWWWWW.

BANG HAMMER OUCH.

BANG HAMMER CRASH.

Mr Potts wasn't very good at putting up pictures.

But, in spite of all the noise, Clarence slumbered on.

By this time Mr Potts was getting rather cross.

"If that parrot doesn't wake me up soon, I'm going to be *very* late for work," he said.

Then he had an idea. He went to his bedroom cupboard and took out his big bass drum.

"I think I'll just have a little practice," he said. And he played on one side of the drum, BOOM BOOM BOOM, and on the other, MOOB MOOB MOOB.

That did it. Clarence's head came out from underneath his wing. He opened two beady eyes and one squawky beak and said, "HAVE A LIE IN, HAVE A LIE IN."

"Have a lie in?" said Mr Potts. "Have a lie in? But you're always telling me to get up."

Clarence blinked his two beady eyes, put his head back underneath his wing and squawked, "BUT NOT ON A SATURDAY."

Peter Potts Has a Difficult Day

Peter Potts the plumber woke up one morning with a horrible headache. It went THUD THUD at the front of his head. It went BOING BOING at the back of his head. And, on top of his head, it went DOINK DOINK DOINK.

Mr Potts got up and wandered about the house groaning, till Clarence squawked, "FRESH AIR FOR A HEADACHE. FRESH AIR FOR A HEADACHE."

"I know, I know," said Mr Potts. "But I haven't got time to go out in the fresh air this morning. I have to install a new pink bathroom suite for old Mrs Hargreaves, and she'll be waiting for me."

So he put his baseball cap carefully on

top of his sore head, and set off in his little red van.

Mrs Hargreaves was watering the geraniums on her bathroom window-ledge when he arrived.

"Ah, there you are, Peter," she said, and turned round with her watering-can and watered Mr Potts as well. "Now I think I've decided how I want you to arrange the new bathroom suite. You can start by putting the bath over by the window. Then I'll be able to read my library book in the bath."

"Right," said Mr Potts, and he heaved the new pink bath over to the window.

As he heaved, his head went THUD BOING DOINK, THUD BOING DOINK.

Mr Potts groaned, but Mrs Hargreaves didn't notice.

"On second thoughts," she said, "it might be a bit draughty by the window. Best move the bath against the far wall instead."

Mr Potts heaved the bath against the far wall.

As he heaved, his head went THUD THUD BOING BOING DOINK DOINK.

Mr Potts groaned again, but Mrs Hargreaves didn't notice. She was too busy worrying about where the pink wash-basin would go.

"Definitely by the window, Peter," she said. "Then, when I take my teeth out to soak, I can pop them in a glass and put them up on the window-ledge for safe keeping."

"Right," said Mr Potts, and he heaved the wash-basin over to the window.

As he heaved, his head went THUD THUD THUD BOING BOING BOING DOINK DOINK DOINK.

Mr Potts groaned even louder, but Mrs Hargreaves didn't notice.

"On second thoughts," she said, "a draught might blow my dentures off the window-ledge and smash them in the wash-basin. Best move the basin behind the door."

Mr Potts heaved the wash-basin behind the door.

As he heaved, his head went THUUUUUUUD BOIOIOIOIOING DOINNNNNNNNNK.

Mr Potts groaned louder still, but Mrs Hargreaves didn't notice. She was too busy worrying about where the pink toilet-bowl would go.

"Definitely by the window," she said. "Then I can sit and do my crossword."

"Right," said Mr Potts, and he heaved the toilet-bowl over to the window.

As he heaved, his head went BANANAS!!!

Mr Potts gave the loudest groan yet, but Mrs Hargreaves still didn't notice. She was deep in thought.

"On second thoughts," she said . . .

And Mr Potts, who was by this time holding his poor head and groaning into the toilet-bowl, said, "Don't tell me. A draught might blow your teeth on to your crossword, then blow your crossword into the bath."

"No, no, don't be silly, Peter," said Mrs Hargreaves. "On second thoughts, I don't think I like the colour of this bathroom suite. Can you come back tomorrow and fit a blue one?"

"All right," agreed Mr Potts, who had decided to take his headache home and put it to bed.

And he went out into the fresh air and took a big deep breath. Then he heaved a great big sigh, and his headache went AWAY.

Happy Birthday, Peter Potts

Peter Potts the plumber woke up early one morning feeling very excited. It was a special day for him. It was his birthday. He jumped out of bed, put on his big blue overalls and his baseball cap, and was on his way downstairs when he heard the cough-cough-splutter of Susie Lee's nurse's car. Mr Potts hurried to open the front door and called to Susie, who was visiting next door.

"Morning, Susie," he said. "Lovely morning, isn't it?"

"Yes," said the nurse. "But you're up very early, Peter. Is something wrong?"

"No, no," said Mr Potts. "But this is a special day for me. Do you know what day it is?"

Susie Lee thought for a moment. "Friday," she said, and hurried into the house next door.

Mr Potts went back indoors. "I think Susie has forgotten it's my birthday," he said to Clarence. The parrot put his head on one side, but said nothing.

Then Mr Potts heard a cheerful whistle coming from outside. "That's Enoch," he said. "I bet he's got lots of birthday cards for me." He ran to the front door and opened it so quickly that Enoch Twyce the postman nearly fell into the hall.

"Morning, Peter," said Enoch. "You're up very early this morning. You must be really keen to get all these bills I have for you."

"Bills?" said Mr Potts. "But there must be more than just bills. This is a special day for me. Do you know what day it is?"

Enoch Twyce thought for a moment. "Pay day," he said, and hurried on to the next house.

Mr Potts went indoors with his bills.

"I think Enoch has forgotten my birthday too," he said to Clarence. The parrot put his head on the other side, but said nothing.

Then Mr Potts heard the noisy rumble of traffic.

"I wonder if PC Sweet is going to direct the traffic this morning," he said, and he opened his sitting-room window and looked out. PC Sweet stood on the edge of the pavement, pulling on a bright orange bib over her policewoman's uniform.

"Morning, Jemima," called Peter Potts. "Lovely morning, isn't it?"

"Yes," said Jemima. "But you're up very early. Is there something wrong?"

"No, no," said Peter Potts. "But this is a special day for me. Do you know what day it is?"

PC Sweet looked at the traffic. "A busy

day," she said, and blew her whistle at a speeding lorry.

Mr Potts closed the window.

"Jemima's forgotten my birthday too," he said to Clarence. The parrot poked his head forward, but still said nothing.

"None of my friends has remembered my birthday," said Mr Potts sadly, and went out to his little red van to start his day's work.

All day long, he tried to be cheerful as he fixed leaky taps, unblocked smelly drains and mended broken gutters. But, although his customers were all very pleasant, nobody knew it was a special day for him, and nobody wished him a happy birthday.

"Oh well," said Mr Potts, when his day's work was done. "I'll just celebrate my birthday by myself. And to cheer myself up, I'll buy a carton of special curry from Mr Gupta's takeaway." And he stopped his little red van outside the shop and went in.

"Oh, I am sorry, Mr Potts," said Mr Gupta, when he heard what was wanted. "But the special curry was finished off this morning, so there isn't any left."

"Oh no," said Mr Potts. "No special curry left, and this is a special day for me too. Do you know what day this is?"

Mr Gupta thought for a moment. "Early closing," he said, and turned the closed sign round on the shop door. "Goodbye now."

Mr Potts went home muttering. "I know what kind of day it is. It's not a special day for me at all. It's a rotten day."

And he threw open his front door, plonked down his tool-bag and went into the sitting-room.

"SURPRISE," squawked Clarence, dancing up and down on his perch.

"HAPPY BIRTHDAY," shouted his friends, jumping up from their chairs and showering him with presents and cards.

"Oh my goodness," said Mr Potts, and he fell back on to a chair under the weight of all the gifts.

Just then the front door opened and Mr Gupta from the takeaway came in, carrying lots of cartons of his special curry.

"This special curry is my present for your birthday tea," he said. "I put it aside for you this morning, specially."

"What a wonderful surprise," said Mr Potts, when he'd finished eating and had opened all his presents. "I can't thank you all enough."

"Well," said Enoch Twyce, "you didn't think your friends would forget your special day, did you?"

Mr Potts looked over at Clarence and winked. "Oh no," he said.

And Clarence winked at him, and threw his head back and squawked, "HAPPY BIRTHDAY, PETER POTTS."